Old Wattles

Old Wattles

by Wynelle Catlin

illustrated by Ron Kuriloff

Doubleday & Company, Inc.
Garden City, New York

Library of Congress cataloging in Publication Data
Catlin, Wynelle.
Old Wattles.
SUMMARY: A Texas farm girl is continually frustrated
by the elusive turkey hen whose eggs she is supposed
to find.
[1. Farm Life—Texas—Fiction. 2. Turkeys—Fiction]
I. Kuriloff, Ron, ill. II. Title.
PZ7.C26950   [Fic]

ISBN 0-385-05114-X   Trade
0-385-05121-2   Prebound
Library of Congress Catalog Card Number 74-26660
Copyright © 1975 by Wynelle Catlin
All Rights Reserved
Printed in the United States of America
First Edition

To my mother,
Dovie Powell Smith

chapter one

Mama took her bonnet from a peg on the cabin wall.

"Eleanore," she said, as she put the bonnet on, "follow Old Wattles today. Find her nest and get her eggs."

"Oh, Mama, do I have to?" Eleanore asked. She tried not to whine. Following the old turkey was a hot, tiring job.

"Yes, you have to," Mama said,

firmly tying the bonnet strings. "A red hen is setting. She can hatch the turkey eggs."

Mama picked up the lunch she'd packed for herself and the boys. She had to help Jake and Samuel in the fields since Papa died. Jake was eighteen and Samuel was sixteen. Mama had to help them get the crops in before it rained.

Mama walked to the cabin door. She looked back at Eleanore before she left.

"Watch Old Wattles good," she said. "We need the eggs."

Eleanore sighed. She was only nine. But she wanted to do her share of the work

Rebecca, Eleanore's older sister, walked into the kitchen. She was carrying a pail of foaming milk. Rebecca was fourteen, almost old enough to

get married. She wore her braids pinned up, not swinging loose like Eleanore's. And Rebecca's dress was as long as Mama's.

Rebecca cooked and cleaned, and did all the work around the cabin. Because she was almost grown up, she thought she could boss Eleanore.

"Are you still sitting?" Rebecca asked. "Mama said you have to follow Old Wattles today."

"I'm going," Eleanore said, jumping up. She put a piece of meat between slices of cold corn bread. She slipped the food into the pocket of her blue-checked gingham dress.

She started to the door. Then she stopped, watching Rebecca strain the milk into a crock jar.

Eleanore wished she didn't have to follow Old Wattles. Following the turkey hen was a hard job. Even helping Rebecca make soap from hog fat and lye was easier than following the turkey.

But Eleanore knew the turkey eggs were important. If she didn't find them, the family wouldn't have turkeys next year.

Old Wattles always hid her nest in the pasture. Every day she went out and laid another egg. She thought if she hid the eggs she'd get to hatch the baby turkeys. Instead, snakes or wild animals ate the eggs or the babies.

When Eleanore found the eggs, Mama would put them under the setting hen to hatch. The chicken hen would take care of the baby turkeys. She'd keep them around the barnyard where they were safe.

If Old Wattles would stay around

the barn, she could hatch her own babies. But the old turkey was too ornery.

"Nora, if you keep standing around, Old Wattles will leave," Rebecca said. She pushed a strand of hair away from her face.

"I'm going," Eleanore said. She flounced her skirt and walked out the door.

"Watch for snakes," Rebecca called after her.

"I always do!" Eleanore declared.

Eleanore had learned about snakes a long time ago. She never stepped over a rock without looking to see if a snake was coiled there. She never stuck her hand into a dark place. Everywhere she went she watched for snakes. Rebecca should know that!

Eleanore glanced down now before

she stepped off the big flat rock doorstep into the warm Texas sun.

She heard the tinkling bell Old Wattles wore around her neck. The turkey might be leaving the barnyard.

Eleanore hurried across the sandy yard to the gate. She climbed to the top.

Old Wattles was in the barnyard with the chickens. She was pecking bits of grain from the ground. With each peck the red wattles on her throat bobbed and wobbled. The bell tinkled sharply.

The sun shining on her brown feathers made them gleam like copper. She raised her head and looked at Eleanore. Her beady black eyes seemed to say, "I'm smarter than you are."

Eleanore hated the contrary old turkey. Why couldn't she lay her eggs in the barn? The black-and-white checkered chicken hens did. The big red hens did, too.

Old Wattles had to be contrary and lay her eggs far in the pasture.

As Eleanore watched, the old turkey hen moved away from the barnyard. She found something good to eat a little way out. Then she found something good a little farther. Gradually, she moved up the side of the small, sloping hill. She pretended she was only looking for food.

She would chase grasshoppers and bugs all the way to her nest. It would take her hours to get there.

Eleanore followed. She didn't get too close. Old Wattles might not go to the nest if she did.

But if Eleanore let Old Wattles get too far away, the old turkey hen would sneak out of sight.

Old Wattles went over the hilltop. Eleanore hurried to the top. Old Wattles was grazing across the flat beyond.

Eleanore stayed behind the turkey. She watched carefully so the turkey wouldn't sneak away.

The sun moved slowly across the sky. Eleanore grew hot and tired. And thirsty. Her throat was so dry it hurt.

She looked at the dark green pecan trees lining the nearby creek. Their shade looked inviting. She wished she had a drink of cool creek water. But she could not go there. If she did, Old Wattles would disappear.

Old Wattles was near a wild plum thicket. She pecked something on the ground. Then she snatched a bug from a weed. Then she chased a flying grasshopper.

Eleanore was tired of watching her peck and snatch and chase. Eleanore was hungry, too. She slipped her hand into her pocket and took out the bread and meat.

Eleanore sat down on a flat rock. It made a nice seat. She watched the turkey as she ate her bread and meat.

She felt something on her foot. Looking down, she saw a red ant. She brushed it away before it could sting her.

Then she saw the ant path through the weeds and grass. Ants hurried along it. Some carried weed seeds. One dragged a grasshopper leg.

Eleanore dropped bread crumbs in the ant path. An ant rushed to a crumb three times his size. He picked it up and staggered down the path. Other ants grabbed smaller crumbs and hurried off. Eleanore watched.

"Oh," she exclaimed as she remembered Old Wattles. She jumped up. The turkey had disappeared.

Eleanore hurried to the plum thicket. She looked all around it. She couldn't find the turkey. And she couldn't hear the bell.

She looked in a clump of sagebrush. She looked everywhere, even places she knew the turkey couldn't be.

She couldn't find the turkey anywhere. Eleanore wanted to cry. But
only babies cry.

She sniffed a few times as she
wearily walked home.

chapter two

"Oh, Becky," Eleanore wailed as she sat on the edge of the front porch. "I looked at some ants. Just for a minute. And Old Wattles disappeared. I can't find her anywhere."

"You'll find her tomorrow," Rebecca said. She got a damp rag. Eleanore washed her face. Rebecca handed her a dipper of cool water. Thankfully, Eleanore gulped it.

"You'd better draw some more water," Rebecca said, looking into the bucket.

Eleanore picked up the bucket. She felt so bad about letting Old Wattles sneak away, she didn't even mind Rebecca telling her what to do.

"I'll have the churn ready when you get through," Rebecca said. She went into the cabin.

Eleanore hurried to the well. Papa had dug it years ago when he built the log cabin. The rock sides were waist high.

She put the bucket on the ground and untied the rope. A wooden bucket was on the end of the rope inside the well. She let the rope down. When it went slack she knew the bucket was filled with water.

Slowly, she pulled on the rope, hand over hand. The overhead pulley

creaked. She drew the bucket of water to the top.

Carefully, she pulled the bucket to the side. She emptied the water into the house bucket.

Then she lowered the well bucket back into the water deep in the well. Mama scolded her if she forgot. If it was left out, the bucket would dry out and crack.

She carried the water to the porch. She set the bucket on the wash shelf beside the wash basin.

She went to the kitchen. Rebecca had a churn of soured milk ready. Eleanore helped Rebecca carry the churn outside to the brush-arbor dairy.

Eleanore liked to sit in the cool dairy. The top was covered with brush, which shaded it. The net wire walls kept animals away and let the breeze come through.

The milk and butter were in covered crocks set in pans of water. The water kept them cool and fresh.

Eleanore plunged the dasher up and down, up and down. Finally, flecks of butter formed on top of the milk. She swirled the dasher gently. The butter gathered in big soft lumps.

"Butter's done, Becky," Eleanore called.

Rebecca came out of the kitchen door with a big bowl and spoon.

"You churn fast," she said. She came into the dairy and knelt beside the churn.

Rebecca dipped the soft butter into the bowl. She beat the butter with the spoon until all the buttermilk was out. Then she poured off the milk. If milk stayed in the butter, the butter would get rancid and taste bad.

"Let me mold, Becky," Eleanore begged.

"All right," Rebecca agreed. She liked to mold butter, too. She was being nice because Eleanore had not found the turkey nest.

Carefully, Eleanore pressed the soft butter into the round wooden mold. When all the butter was in, she put the mold upside down on the butter plate. She pushed the plunger. The butter came out. The plunger had stamped a flower design in the center of the round butter.

"That's pretty," Rebecca exclaimed. She and Eleanore put the milk and butter in the water pans to keep cool.

Eleanore helped Rebecca all afternoon. She did everything Rebecca told her to. She didn't fuss once.

She even mixed the corn bread for supper. She had just taken it from the oven when the sound of jingling harness told her Mama and the boys were in from the fields.

Eleanore was busy setting plates on the table when Mama came into the kitchen. Eleanore couldn't look up.

"Eleanore, did you find the turkey est?" Mama asked.

"No, ma'am," Eleanore answered. She didn't want to look at Mama. She didn't want to see the disappointment in Mama's face.

Rebecca put a plate of fried ham and a bowl of milk gravy on the table. Eleanore got the hot corn bread.

Jake's and Samuel's heavy boots sounded on the front porch. Water sloshed as they washed in the basin.

The kitchen seemed small when Jake walked into it. He was so tall that Eleanore looked way up to see his face. His straight black hair was neatly combed.

"Hi, little sister," he said warmly.

Samuel, just as tall but slimmer, crowded into the room behind Jake. His brown hair stuck up all over his head.

"Samuel, comb your hair," Mama said sternly.

"I did, Mama," Samuel protested. He smoothed his unruly hair with his hands.

"He did, Mama," Jake said earnestly. He always defended Samuel when Mama scolded.

"All right," Mama said finally.

Samuel crowded past Jake. He slid onto the bench beside Eleanore.

"What's my little sister been doing today? Playing?" he asked. He always teased.

"No," Eleanore said. She ducked her head. Watching ants wasn't really playing, just forgetting. She didn't tell Samuel she had let Old Wattles sneak away.

Jake, Mama, and Rebecca pulled straight-backed chairs to the table.

"Samuel, if you're through teasing Eleanore, you can say the blessing," Mama said crisply.

They bowed their heads.

"Dear Lord," Samuel prayed, "bless this food we put in our mouths to feed our bodies. Let us be thankful we have this food. And let us get the crops in before it rains so we'll have some more. Amen."

They raised their heads. Mama looked hard at Samuel. Was he making fun? Or was he serious?

Mama must have decided he was serious. She picked up the plate of ham and took a piece. She passed the plate to Jake.

Playfully, Samuel stuck out his elbows. He pushed Eleanore to the end of the bench.

"Got to have lots of room to eat," he said.

"Stop," Eleanore protested. But she laughed. She grabbed his arm and shoved back. She couldn't budge him.

"Samuel," Mama warned.

"Nora churned the butter and molded it," Rebecca said quickly. "And made the corn bread."

"That's right pretty butter," Jake said. He took some from the side so he wouldn't ruin the flower print in the middle. He spread the butter on a slice of hot corn bread. When it had melted to a shiny yellow liquid, he took a large bite.

"Bread's good, too," he declared. Eleanore was pleased. But Jake would have said it was good even if it hadn't been.

Then Jake and Samuel were too busy eating to talk. Mama looked too tired.

Jake sopped the last bit of gravy from his plate with a piece of bread. He leaned back in his chair.

"We sure got good sisters," he declared.

"Good for what?" Samuel asked. Eleanore knew he was teasing. But it was better to hear nice words.

Samuel looked at her face. He hugged her.

"Well, maybe for making butter and cooking corn bread," he said. "After that supper, I feel like fiddling."

"Oh, good," Eleanore exclaimed. Samuel hadn't fiddled in a long time. She jumped up and began clearing the table.

Samuel went through the front room. He took Papa's fiddle from beside the fireplace. He, Mama, and Jake went out on the dark front porch. Samuel tuned the fiddle.

Eleanore and Rebecca hurried to put up the table. They carried the dirty dishes to the cabinet. Rebecca washed them in a pan of water.

Eleanore wiped the table top. She put clean spoons into the spoon holder that stayed on the table. The salt and pepper shakers were full. The molasses pitcher was, too. She arranged all the things neatly in the center of the table. She covered them with a clean cloth.

Together she and Rebecca dried the dishes. Then they hurried to the porch.

In the dim light, Eleanore could barely see Mama sitting in a chair. Jake and Samuel sat on the edge of the porch. They leaned against the posts, one on either side.

Rebecca and Eleanore sat down. They dangled their legs off the edge of the porch.

Then Eleanore remembered the big rattlesnake curled beside the porch one day. She had seen it as she started to step down. She had screamed. Jake had come running and killed it.

Eleanore's feet tingled as she re-membered the snake. She drew her feet up onto the porch and spread her skirt over them

A cool breeze was blowing. She looked up at the black sky. Millions of stars were twinkling.

Samuel played a rollicking tune. Then another and another. Eleanore felt good inside. Samuel and the fiddle made beautiful music.

"Let's all sing," Rebecca said.

From the fiddle strings came the notes of "Onward, Christian soldiers, marching as to war."

Lustily, Eleanore sang out the words with the others. As the song ended, Eleanore turned to Mama.

"Sing for us," she said softly. She hadn't heard Mama sing since Papa died.

Mama began singing about a letter edged in black, a letter that brought a sad message.

Samuel followed softly on the fiddle as Mama's clear, sweet voice sang, "But he little knew the sorrow that he brought me when he handed me the letter edged in black . . .

"Letter edged in black,
  Letter edged in black.
  Oh, he little knew the sorrow . . ."

Tears choked Mama's voice. She couldn't keep singing. Mama was thinking of Papa. Eleanore was thinking of him, too.

Quickly, Samuel began playing one of Papa's happy songs. Keeping time with his foot, Samuel sang as he fiddled,

"Raccoon up a 'simmon tree.
  Possum on the ground.
  Possum says, you son of a gun,
  Shake them 'simmons down."

Eleanore laughed and clapped her hands. She could be happy, too, thinking about Papa. Eleanore sang the next verse with Samuel,

"Raccoon's tail's ringed all around.
Possum's tail is bare.
Rabbit has no tail at all.
But a little bunch of hair."

Mama, Jake, and Rebecca applauded.

"More, more," Jake said.

"Nope, that's all," Samuel said, standing up.

Eleanore hated to quit singing. She felt warm and good sitting on the dark porch singing. For a little while she had forgotten she would have to follow Old Wattles again tomorrow.

chapter three

"Nora. Nora."

Faintly, Eleanore heard Rebecca calling. She wanted to go back to sleep.

Slowly, she opened her eyes. She shivered in the cool morning air. The wooden window shutters of the loft room were open.

Through the window came sounds of jingling harness. Jake was yelling "gee-up" to the mules.

Eleanore had overslept. She jumped up. She ran to the window.

Jake was driving the mules through the back gate. Samuel and Mama followed him. Eleanore wished Mama didn't have to work in the fields.

Quickly Eleanore slipped into her dress. She ran down the narrow stairs. She crossed the main room of the cabin and hurried into the lean-to kitchen.

"You're a laze-a-bed," Rebecca teased.

"Why didn't you wake me?" Eleanore asked. "You know I have to follow that old turkey again."

"You have plenty of time," Rebecca answered. She spooned cornmeal mush into Eleanore's favorite blue-flowered bowl.

"Mama says for you to sweep the yard, too," Rebecca added.

Eleanore sat down at the table. Rebecca put the bowl of mush in front of her. Eleanore put butter on it. Then she added a spoonful of honey.

Jake had robbed a bee tree last fall. Now the family had lots of sweet honey.

She took a bite of mush. She let it slide down her throat. It tasted so good.

Rebecca was washing dishes.

"I've got to find that old turkey's nest today, Becky," Eleanore said. She wanted to cry just thinking about having to follow Old Wattles.

"You'll find it today," Rebecca assured her, "if you don't stop to watch ants."

Eleanore didn't intend to watch ants. But following the old turkey wasn't easy. If Rebecca had to do it, she'd know how hard it was.

Rebecca walked to the table. Her hands dripped dishwater.

"Hurry now," she said. "I have to wash the bowl. And you have to make the beds."

Rebecca was always telling her what to do. Slowly, Eleanore scooped the last bit of mush into her mouth. Rebecca took the bowl.

Eleanore went through the front room. Mama's bed was here. But Mama made her own bed each morning.

Eleanore had to make the boys' bed. Their tiny lean-to room was to one side of the front porch. She went in. She straightened the wrinkled covers. She plumped the goose-down pillows.

She could hear Old Wattles' bell

tinkling. Eleanore went outside. She looked. The turkey was still in the barnyard.

She might have time to sweep the yard before Old Wattles left for her nest. She went to the chimney corner for the yard broom. Mama had made the broom by tying clumps of broom-weed to the end of a stick.

Papa used to tease Mama. He said she was more particular about the yard being swept than the floors.

But that wasn't true. Mama liked everything to be neat and clean. She even put on a clean apron each morning to work in the fields.

Carefully, Eleanore brushed the twigs and leaves from the sandy yard. She heard Old Wattles' bell tinkling up the hill. She hadn't finished the far corner of the yard. But she couldn't wait.

She put the broom back in the chimney corner and called to Rebecca, "I'm going."

She climbed over the barnyard gate. Old Wattles was going over the hill. Eleanore ran to the top. Old Wattles was in the flat below.

Eleanore followed her slowly. The long tiring hours passed.

Old Wattles found choice weeds in one direction. She chased grasshoppers in another. She found tidbits on the ground in still another.

But all the time the turkey was going the same way she'd gone yesterday.

Suddenly Old Wattles stopped. She looked at something on the ground. She began making the whirring noise turkeys make when they're alarmed.

Eleanore waited. If she ran up and

Old Wattles had only found a lizard, the turkey would get excited. She might decide not to lay an egg today. She might go back to the barnyard.

Old Wattles kept whirring. She spread her wings. She drummed the ground with her feet.

Eleanore walked closer. Suddenly she heard the chilling rattle of an angry rattlesnake. She shivered with cold chill bumps.

Old Wattles hated snakes. She ruffled her feathers and got ready to fight.

"Leave it alone, Wattles! Leave it alone!" Eleanore screamed. The turkey paid no attention.

Eleanore moved closer. The snake was coiled. The square ugly head was held high. It was ready to strike. Its rattles buzzed constantly.

Old Wattles rushed at the rattler, pecking and clawing. The snake struck at her. It missed by inches.

The turkey moved back, and then attacked again. The angry snake struck again and again. It barely missed Old Wattles each time.

Eleanore screamed at the turkey. If the snake buried its fangs in Old Wattles' neck, the poison would kill her. Then the family wouldn't have Old Wattles *or* her eggs.

Eleanore was so scared she was sick. She wanted to run to the fields for Jake and Samuel. But that would take too long.

She had to do something. She looked for a weapon. She found a heavy stick. It was too short. If she got close enough to hit the snake, the snake could bite her.

Eleanore saw a rock. Sometimes she could hit things with rocks. She picked it up.

When Old Wattles saw Eleanore coming with the rock, she backed away.

The angry snake turned its ugly head toward Eleanore. The rattles buzzed shrilly.

Eleanore's feet and legs tingled. She could imagine the snake's fangs sinking into her flesh.

Eleanore moved as close as she dared. She held the rock with shaking hands. She held it high over her head. She flung it as hard as she could.

The snake ducked. The rock missed. Eleanore backed away. Old Wattles stood nearby. She acted as if she wanted to fight again.

"Go away," Eleanore yelled at the turkey. "Go away!"

Old Wattles just looked at Eleanore with beady eyes. She whirred her alarm noise.

Eleanore looked around desperately. She found another rock.

She aimed the rock and threw it with all her might.

The rock hit the snake. The snake was stunned. Eleanore grabbed up the stick and clubbed the snake.

Her knees were so weak they barely held her up. She breathed a sigh of relief. Then she remembered that Jake always said, "Where you find one snake, you'll find another."

She looked around for another snake. She didn't see one.

Where was Old Wattles? Eleanore

looked. The turkey hen was trotting back to the barnyard.

Eleanore's legs were still weak. But she ran behind as fast as she could.

chapter four

"Becky, Becky!" Eleanore screamed as she ran into the yard.

Rebecca came running.

"What's the matter?" Rebecca asked. She was frightened.

"A snake, Becky. A big snake," Eleanore cried.

"Where did it bite you?" Frantically, Rebecca searched for fang marks.

"No, no," Eleanore exclaimed, "it didn't bite me. I killed it."

Rebecca hugged Eleanore in relief.

"You're not hurt," Rebecca said gratefully. "You scared me so."

Rebecca sat beside Eleanore until Eleanore felt better.

"You'd better finish sweeping the yard," Rebecca said, jumping up.

"I was going to," Eleanore said.

Rebecca always told her what to do.

Eleanore's knees were still trembly. She went to the chimney corner and got the broom. She swept the rest of the yard. The broom made a striped wavy pattern. The sand was neat and pretty.

But right in the middle of the yard were Eleanore's bare footprints. She brushed them out. She walked backward. She brushed until she got to the chimney corner.

Eleanore looked at the neat yard. How would she get on the porch without making more footprints? She tip-toed close to the cabin wall. She looked back. Only her toe prints showed. They didn't show very much.

She went inside. Rebecca had scraps of material laid out on Mama's bed. She was getting ready to piece a quilt.

"Want to help?" Rebecca asked. She picked up a piece of blue-checked gingham.

"Here's your dress," Rebecca said.

"And here's yours," Eleanore said. She picked up a piece of pink print calico.

There were scraps from all their dresses. And Mama's dresses. And Jake's and Samuel's shirts.

Rebecca was matching colors. She picked up a scrap of solid green. She held it beside a print with green leaves.

"These look pretty together," she said. Eleanore agreed.

Together they matched a pink check with the pink print. They matched a solid blue with the blue check. They put the colors together until Rebecca said there was enough for a quilt.

She got the quilt pattern and the scissors. She put the pattern on each piece of material. Carefully, she cut around the edges.

She wouldn't let Eleanore cut the pieces. But she gave Eleanore scraps to make an apron for the rag doll.

Eleanore sewed the apron while Rebecca cut out and sewed quilt blocks. The afternoon passed quickly.

Mama didn't scold that night at the supper table.

"It wasn't your fault Old Wattles tangled with a snake," Mama said wearily. "But follow her again tomorrow."

"Nora, you be careful fighting rattlesnakes as big as you are," Samuel teased. But his eyes looked concerned.

After supper, Samuel went to the pasture and cut the snake's rattles off. He brought them to the house and held them up for everyone to see.

"Fourteen rattles. Biggest snake anyone's killed around here," he said.

He tied a string on the rattles. He hung them on the porch. Other rattles were hanging there.

Eleanore didn't tell anyone how scared she had been.

"Listen, snake-fighter, I don't want you to tackle that new bull," Jake said gravely. "You shouldn't take any chances. Keep far away from him."

"I will," Eleanore promised. Jake didn't have to worry. One time Eleanore had seen a bull trample a dog. The bull had stomped and stomped the dog. Then he'd caught the dog with his horns and thrown it high into the air.

Eleanore was tired. She could hardly stay awake until bedtime.

When she went to sleep she had nightmares. Snakes chased her. Then bulls chased her. She would run as fast as she could. But she didn't go anywhere. Then as a snake or bull nearly caught her, she would wake up. She was scared even after she knew that it was only a dream. And that she was in her own bed.

The snakes and bulls didn't get as tired as she did. They took turns.

chapter five

Eleanore was cross the next morning. She grumbled to herself as she made the beds.

The breakfast oatmeal was burned. It tasted terrible. Eleanore complained. Tears came to Rebecca's eyes. She turned her head away.

"I'm sorry," Eleanore muttered. But she was so cross she really didn't feel sorry. She knew Rebecca did all

the housework. But Eleanore had to
follow the old turkey. That was hard,
too.

She put meat and bread in her
pocket. She hurried to the barnyard.
She looked at Old Wattles, thinking
how ugly the turkey was.

The turkey looked at Eleanore.

"Gobble, gobble," she said, her wattles bobbing.

"Gobble, gobble, yourself," Eleanore answered crossly.

When Old Wattles began grazing up the hill, Eleanore followed. The hours passed slower than ever.

Old Wattles went through a mesquite thicket. Eleanore pushed her way through the bushy trees. The thorny limbs caught at her clothes. They scratched her arms and hands.

Old Wattles found the dead snake. She clucked and whirred over the body. Eleanore passed around. She didn't want to look at it. But she watched for its mate. The mate might be coiled nearby.

Eleanore saw the cattle. She watched for the bull. She didn't see him. The cattle grazed in the other direction.

She watched the turkey so hard her eyes hurt. The sun was hot. Eleanore was tired and thirsty. And hungry.

Today she wouldn't sit down to eat. She might be tempted to watch ants. She took the bread and meat from her pocket. She ate standing up.

She didn't let her eyes wander from Old Wattles. She took the last bite and started after the turkey again. She didn't see the rock sticking out of the ground. She stubbed her toe. She fell.

"Oh," she cried with pain as she grabbed her skinned knee.

"Oh," she cried as she saw her broken toenail and bloody toe.

"Oh," she cried as she remembered the turkey. She jumped up. She looked. Old Wattles had been close to the plum thicket. She had disappeared.

Eleanore limped to the thicket. She looked and looked. She couldn't find the turkey.

Her toe hurt. Her knee hurt. And she felt bad inside. Slowly the tears rolled down her cheeks.

She brushed them away. She looked again for the turkey. She looked and looked until there was no other place to look.

Wearily, she limped home.

"Oh, Nora," Rebecca cried. "What happened today?"

Eleanore told her. Rebecca got a pan of water and some clean white rags.

Gently, she washed Eleanore's foot and knee. She tore a long narrow strip from a clean rag. She wound the strip around Eleanore's sore toe. She tied it with a big bow.

"There," she said, laughing.

Rebecca was trying to make Eleanore feel better. Her toe did feel better. But inside she didn't.

"Becky, what will I do? I have to find that turkey nest," Eleanore wailed.

"Tomorrow, I'll help you," Rebecca offered. "Together we can keep that old turkey from sneaking away from us."

Eleanore was relieved. She knew Rebecca could find the turkey. Rebecca could do anything.

Eleanore thought of all the things Rebecca did every day. Rebecca worked hard. Everyone worked hard.

Eleanore said slowly, "Finding the eggs is my job. I'll find the nest tomorrow."

Eleanore helped Rebecca all afternoon. She did everything Rebecca asked her to.

She hated to hear the jingling harness that evening.

Mama took one look at Eleanore's

face. She said tiredly, "You didn't find the turkey nest."

"It wasn't her fault, Mama," Rebecca said quickly. "She fell down and skinned her knee. And hurt her toe. I tied it up."

Silently Mama inspected the toe and knee.

"I'm sorry, Mama," Eleanore said.

"I know you didn't mean to fall down, Eleanore," Mama said sternly. "But you have to be careful. You know how important it is to find the eggs."

"I know, Mama," Eleanore said. She wanted to cry. "I'll find them tomorrow. I promise I will."

chapter six

———◆———

Eleanore was tired when she woke up. She could hardly get out of bed. She stumbled as she did her usual chores.

Rebecca asked her to get water before she followed Old Wattles. Eleanore thought her arms would fall off before she drew the bucket to the top of the well.

Old Wattles' bell tinkled up the

hillside. Eleanore followed. All morning she never took her eyes off the turkey.

As Old Wattles neared the plum thicket, Eleanore saw some cattle. She didn't see the bull with them.

She wasn't afraid of the cows. The cows knew Eleanore. She helped throw hay to them in winter. Then she had to be careful. They hurried to eat and nearly stepped on her. But the only time one tried to fight was when it had a new calf.

The cows had their heads lowered, eating grass.

Eleanore wasn't afraid. But she didn't go through the middle of the herd as Old Wattles did. The turkey pecked the ground under one of the cows. The cow ignored her.

Eleanore went around the cows. She kept her eyes on the turkey.

Then one of the cows raised its head. It wasn't a cow. It was the bull!

Eleanore was too close. The bull eyed her. He lowered his head and shook his horns. He pawed the ground. The dirt flew into the air.

Eleanore's heart pounded. She stood still. Maybe he was bluffing. If she didn't move, he might decide she was not a threat.

But the bull wasn't bluffing. He bellowed and charged. Eleanore turned. She ran toward the nearest tree.

She felt as if she were running hard but not going anywhere. Her lungs were bursting. Her ears roared. She thought she could feel the bull's breath on her back. She didn't dare look back. She might trip and fall.

Eleanore neared the tree. She

leaped the last few feet. She grabbed a limb. She clawed and scrambled onto the limb.

The bull bellowed his rage. He pawed the ground under the tree. He threw his massive head into the air. Foam from his nostrils sprayed Eleanore.

She grabbed another limb. She climbed higher. She held onto the tree trunk with weak, trembling arms.

The angry bull pawed the ground. He sent dirt and leaves high into the air. He looked up at her and bellowed loudly.

Eleanore felt weak and dizzy. She held tightly to the tree. She hoped she wouldn't fall under his feet. He would stomp her to death.

The bull stayed under the tree for a

long time. The cows had watched the chase with interest. But Eleanore sitting in a tree was not exciting to them. They went back to their grazing. Slowly, they moved away.

The bull looked at the cows. He looked at Eleanore in the tree. He pawed the ground. He didn't want to leave her. But he didn't want the cows to leave him.

Finally, he trotted over to the cows. He kept looking at Eleanore. If Eleanore climbed down, he would be back.

Eleanore didn't even look for Old Wattles. She knew the turkey had disappeared.

Eleanore sat on the hard tree limb. She held the trunk tightly. A few tears came out of her eyes. Then she sobbed loudly.

She wondered how long she would

have to stay in the tree. Maybe forever, until she turned to part of the
tree.

Would they call it an Eleanore
tree? Persimmon trees had persim-
mons in them. Pecan trees had
pecans. Mesquite trees had mesquite
beans.

She got lonesome thinking about
staying in the tree forever. She cried
again.

She wouldn't have to stay forever.
Samuel and Jake would come looking
for her tonight. But then the bull
would trample them. And throw
them into the air with his horns.

After a long time, the cows went
over the hill. The bull looked in her
direction. Then he followed them.

Eleanore's arms and legs were so
stiff she could hardly climb down. She
kept an eye on the hilltop. The bull

might decide to come back. Her feet touched the ground. She made a bee-line for the pasture fence. She got on the other side.

She went around the barn and sheds. She ran to the cabin.

"Becky! Oh, Becky!" she cried. She flung herself into her sister's arms. She cried so hard she couldn't tell Rebecca what was wrong. Rebecca was alarmed. She threatened to get Mama.

Eleanore stopped crying. She told Rebecca about the bull chasing her.

Rebecca petted her.

"Go to bed for a while," she urged.

Eleanore didn't want to go upstairs by herself. She stayed beside Rebecca all afternoon.

That evening Rebecca had to tell Mama, Jake, and Samuel about the bull. Eleanore couldn't. She nearly cried just thinking about it.

"The bull has to go," Jake said sternly. "Come on, Sam. We'll put him in the trap pasture. Then we'll sell him first chance we get."

Jake and Samuel took vicious bull-whips. They went to round up the bull.

When they came back, Jake said, "The bull is in the trap. Don't go near it, Nora."

"I won't," Eleanore promised.

Mama had been quiet all evening.

"Eleanore, you'd best not follow the turkey again," Mama said. "But we need the eggs. I'll follow Old Wattles tomorrow. You boys will have to do without me."

"Wait till the next day and I'll follow her," Samuel offered.

"You know we don't work on the

Lord's day, Samuel," Mama said
sternly.

"Just once won't hurt, Mama. Be-
sides, following the turkey is not
really work," Samuel protested.

"Your Papa didn't hold with doing

anything on the Sabbath. Not even just once." Mama's mouth was set firm. Samuel knew not to argue.

"I'll find the nest tomorrow, Mama," Eleanore said.

"No. You've had plenty of time," Mama said. "I'll find it myself."

Eleanore felt bad. All the others did their share of work. And she couldn't even find the turkey eggs. Mama wouldn't let her try again.

chapter seven

The next morning clouds hung heavy
overhead. Mama stood at the cabin
door. She looked at the threatening
sky. The crops had to be in before it
rained.

"Mama," Eleanore said timidly. "I
can find the nest today. I know I can if
you'll let me try again."

Mama looked at the rain clouds.
She looked at Eleanore. Eleanore

held her breath. Finally, Mama said, "It's best I help the boys before it rains. You find the turkey nest today."

Mama hugged Eleanore.

"But mind, you be careful," Mama said sternly. She went out the door.

Eleanore fixed meat and bread for her lunch. She hurried to the barnyard. She followed Old Wattles up the hill and across the flat.

Eleanore was glad the sun wasn't shining. At least it wasn't hot. She followed closer than she'd ever followed. The turkey didn't make a single move that Eleanore didn't see.

Old Wattles passed the dead rattlesnake. Eleanore started around. She stopped. Her heart jumped into her mouth. A long snake's body lay hidden by weeds. Was it the rattlesnake's mate?

The snake moved through the weeds. What would Eleanore do? She didn't have time for another fight. Old Wattles would sneak away.

The snake glided into Eleanore's path. With relief, she saw it was a harmless black bullsnake, not a rattler. He was looking for mice to eat. She let him crawl on his way.

The cows were grazing in the flat. Eleanore knew the bull was penned. She could hear his far-off bellowing.

Eleanore didn't get hot and thirsty as the slow hours passed. But she got hungry. Her stomach rumbled with hunger. But she wouldn't eat. She wouldn't do anything that might make her lose sight of the turkey.

Old Wattles neared the plum thicket. Eleanore stared hard at the turkey. Old Wattles disappeared.

Eleanore blinked her eyes. She

couldn't believe the turkey had disappeared. But she was gone. She was nowhere in sight.

Eleanore ran to the thicket. She looked all around it. She couldn't find Old Wattles.

She listened. She couldn't hear the bell. Old Wattles wasn't moving. She was on her nest.

But where was the nest? Eleanore looked everywhere the turkey could be. She couldn't find the turkey anywhere.

She stood, thinking. Old Wattles had disappeared in front of the plum thicket. She had to be in it.

Eleanore went to the thicket. She got down on her hands and knees. Watching for angry rattlesnakes or silent copperheads, she crawled around the thicket. She looked into the branches.

She couldn't find the turkey. But she couldn't give up. She *had* to find the turkey.

She parted some branches and peered into them. She looked right at Old Wattles.

The old turkey hen drew her head back. Her beady eyes glared at Eleanore.

"I found you, you sneaky old turkey," Eleanore exclaimed happily.

The hen was sitting on the nest she'd hidden so cleverly. Her brown feathers blended with the brown branches of the plum bushes. Two feet away Eleanore couldn't see the turkey. No wonder she hadn't been able to find the nest before!

Eleanore went to a nearby tree and sat down in the shade. She had to wait for Old Wattles to lay her egg. When she left the nest, Eleanore could get the eggs.

Mama would put them under the setting hen to hatch. Then the chicken hen would tend the fuzzy baby turkeys. She'd cluck to them. They would run around cheeping their baby turkey sounds.

Then the turkeys would grow bigger than the red hen. But they would still follow as she clucked to them.

Eleanore smiled thinking about it.

Eleanore was hungry. She took out her bread and meat. She ate it. She wished she had some more.

She decided she could have laid a dozen eggs in the time it took Old Wattles to lay one.

Finally, she heard the turkey's bell tinkling on the far side of the thicket. The contrary old turkey knew Eleanore had found her nest. But she still sneaked out of the thicket.

Eleanore ran to the thicket. She pushed aside the scratchy branches. Fifteen big brown-speckled eggs were in the nest.

She gathered up her skirt with one hand. She made a basket. Carefully, she placed the eggs in it.

She walked slowly and carefully.

She watched every step so she wouldn't fall down. She walked slowly across the pasture.

The clouds overhead grew darker. It looked as if rain would fall any minute. But she didn't walk faster. She was not going to break the eggs.

She neared the cabin.

"Becky, Becky!" she called loudly.

Rebecca came running through the door. She was frightened. But when she saw Eleanore's careful steps and skirt basket, she knew Eleanore had found the eggs. She jumped up and down.

"You found them, you found them!" she exclaimed. Then she said, "Don't fall down. Don't bump them. Don't break them."

"I carried them all this way," Eleanore told Rebecca. "And I didn't break a single one."

But Eleanore guessed Rebecca would always tell her what to do.

"Let's put them in a bowl," Rebecca said. She ran into the cabin. She came back with a huge bowl and put it on the porch. Carefully, they took the eggs from Eleanore's skirt. They put them in the bowl. The bowl was full. Fifteen turkey eggs were a lot of eggs!

Rebecca grabbed Eleanore's hands. They danced around the clean sandy yard.

A raindrop splashed on the end of Eleanore's nose. Rain spattered lightly in the sand of the yard.

They stopped dancing. They looked toward the fields. Had Mama and the boys gotten the crops in?

They heard the sound of jingling harness. Jake and Samuel rushed the mules and the loaded wagon to the

barn. Mama hurried to the house.

"We finished just as it began
sprinkling," she said. Then she saw
the bowl of turkey eggs.

"And you found Old Wattles' nest!" she exclaimed. She stepped up on the porch. She picked up the big bowl of eggs.

Larger raindrops splashed Eleanore and Rebecca. The girls hurried to the shelter of the porch.

Jake and Samuel ran from the barn. Just as they jumped onto the porch, a cloudburst poured down. Rain drummed loudly on the roof.

"Say, look at all the turkey eggs," Jake said.

"Yes, Eleanore found the nest. Now we can set them." Mama looked happy.

"Nora, I think you need a bath," Samuel declared. He grabbed her and pretended to push her from the porch into the pouring rain.

"Stop," Eleanore protested. But she laughed happily.

Samuel stuck his hand into the rain. He dripped water on Eleanore's head.

"Samuel, quit teasing," Mama scolded. But she didn't sound as if she minded.

"Look," Rebecca said, pointing.

Old Wattles was hurrying from the pasture. Rain splashed on her. Her wet feathers dragged in the mud. She looked cross and disgusted.

Poor Old Wattles. She looked funny hurrying through the rain toward the barn.

Eleanore laughed. Jake, Samuel, and Rebecca laughed.

Mama was still holding the bowl of turkey eggs. She laughed, too.

WYNELLE CATLIN grew up on a farm and has lived most of her life in Jack County in north central Texas. She has worked on a local newspaper, directed a day-care center, and served as an elementary school auxiliary teacher. In recent years she has written historical articles about the West, and has begun writing books for children.

The idea for *Old Wattles,* her first children's book, came from the experiences of her Aunt Bert, whose job it was to follow the turkey hens on the farm and find their eggs. Old Wattles was modeled after "all the contrary old turkey hens" from Wynelle Catlin's own childhood. She and her husband have three grown children and one teen-aged son still at home. They live "quietly in the country," where, in addition to writing, Wynelle Catlin churns milk, and makes cottage cheese, butter, and jellies and jams.